Two outs.

Runners at second and third.

The Dodgers were two runs down with the runners in scoring position.

But Harlan was coming up to bat.

He bit down on his bottom lip so hard it hurt. He told himself to forget everything that had happened before.

This was it.

It all came down to *right now*.

Look for these books about the
Angel Park All-Stars

BIG BASE HIT

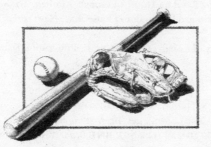

By Dean Hughes

Illustrated by Dennis Lyall

Bullseye Books • Alfred A. Knopf
New York

DR. M. JERRY WEISS, Distinguished Service Professor of Communications at Jersey City State College, is the educational consultant for Bullseye Books. A past chair of the International Reading Association President's Advisory Committee on Intellectual Freedom, he travels frequently to give workshops on the use of trade books in schools.

Library of Congress Cataloging-in-Publication Data
Hughes, Dean, 1943–
Big base hit / by Dean Hughes ; illustrated by Dennis Lyall.
p.   cm.—(Angel Park all-stars ; 2)
Summary: Harlan Sloan, a rookie on the Little League baseball team, gets his first big base hit.
ISBN 0-679-80427-7 (pbk.)   ISBN 0-679-90427-1 (lib. bdg.)
[1. Baseball—Fiction]   I. Lyall, Dennis, ill.   II. Title.
III. Series: Hughes, Dean, 1943–   Angel Park all-stars ; 2.
PZ7.H87312Bi   1990
[Fic]—dc20   89-37875

RL: 4.4

First Bullseye Books edition: April 1990
Manufactured in the United States of America
1   2   3   4   5   6   7   8   9   10

for Jacob Hill

★ 1 ★

Everybody Hits

"That ball is *out of here!*" Jacob Scott yelled.

Kenny had hit a screaming line drive that kept right on going until it dropped over the left-field fence. The Dodgers were already ahead of the A's 3 to 0 and it was only the first inning.

Harlan Sloan ran from the dugout with all the other Dodgers. He waited his chance to give Kenny a leaping high-five. Jacob did the same, and the three rookies trotted back to the dugout.

Things were looking good. The Dodgers had won the first two games of the season, and now they seemed to be on the way to the third. "We're going *all the way* this year," Henry White yelled. "We got a third-grader who hits home runs!"

"*YEAH!!!!*" a bunch of the players yelled.

When Harlan took his seat on the bench again, he tried to picture himself doing his own home-run trot. He wished he were one more third-grader who could knock a ball that far.

He was big for his age and strong—like Kenny. So what if he seemed to be all elbows and knees? Maybe he *would* do it sometime. And if he did, maybe Rodney Bunson and the other older guys would get off his back.

Bunson was stepping up to bat now. He had threatened to quit the team after the last game. But here he was . . . hoping to be the star again. And Kenny had already stolen the show.

Whack. Bunson slammed the first pitch into left-center.

"*Everybody* hits today," Jenny Roper shouted.

Billy Bacon, the Dodgers' stout little

catcher, yelled, "That pitcher has no arm. It's like batting practice out there."

"What a start for the Dodgers!" Jacob Scott announced. He was pretending to hold a microphone. "Sandoval has blasted one over the fence and Burner Bunson, pitcher and power-hitter, has kept the rally going."

Sterling Malone, the Dodgers' left fielder, stepped to the plate. He was a strong fifth-grader who could really hit, too.

"Holy smoke, fans," Jacob announced, "the A's may never come to bat today. It's only a couple more hours until sundown."

All the Dodgers laughed, and then they cheered when Sterling hammered the ball past the second baseman.

Bunson scored. Four to nothing and still no outs.

"Come on, Jenny," everyone was yelling. "Keep it going."

And she did.

Jenny Roper cracked a hard grounder that skittered past the bag before the first baseman could move. It went for a double and Sterling scored all the way from first.

Five to nothing and counting.

"I know what A's stands for," Billy Bacon yelled. "But my mom won't let me say that word."

Everyone was laughing, even some of the Dodgers' parents behind the dugout.

This was fun.

It was a warm evening. The sky was turning dark blue as the sun angled toward the desert horizon. Everyone in Angel Park seemed to be at the game. It was perfect—except that Harlan wanted to get in the game and get a base hit of his own.

Jacob, the other third-grader on the team along with Harlan and Kenny, sat down next to Harlan. "We can hit this guy," he said. "I can't wait to get in the game." He smiled, showing the funny-looking split between his front teeth.

"Yeah, me too."

"You got your first hit last game," Jacob said. "I think I'll get mine today."

"Mine wasn't a real hit," Harlan said. "It

was just a bunt. This time I want to knock one across the street."

"We will. Both of us will today."

But Jeff Reinhold didn't. He hit a looper to second base. Jenny had taken off for third. The second baseman threw to the shortstop and doubled her off before she could get back.

And then Billy Bacon found out that some of the A's could play ball. He hit a high fly to center field, and the center fielder—a little guy who could really go—made a nice running catch.

The Dodgers' rally was suddenly over.

Jacob and Harlan watched their infielders warm up. Henry White, the third baseman for the Dodgers, fielded a ground ball perfectly, smoothly, and fired to first—right on target.

"Do you think we'll be that good when we're the older guys?" Jacob asked.

"We'll be better," Harlan said, grinning. "But I want to do something now. Kenny's already one of the best."

"He got off to a fast start because his dad

was a major leaguer and helped him so much," Jacob said. "We'll catch up."

Harlan thought so too. In fact, he thought he might start catching up today. He couldn't wait to get in the game.

The first batter for the A's hit a little nubber of a ground ball back to Bunson. The next batter struck out.

The third batter was the A's star—a guy named Jared Bessant. He played third base and was really fast. But Bunson got a two-and-two count on him, and then he threw his hardest fastball right on by him.

The Dodgers were back up and soon scoring runs again. They batted around, pushing across five more runs before the A's changed pitchers. And that didn't stop the Dodgers, either.

When Bunson hit the second homer of the game—another three-run shot—the Dodgers were ahead 16 to 0.

Coach Wilkens finally showed some mercy. He walked over to the dugout. "Jacob, bat for Sterling," the coach said.

He jumped up and hurried out to find a

bat. But when Jacob got up to bat, Harlan could see that he was trying way too hard. He looked like a little kid compared to the big catcher, but he swung like he wanted to kill the ball.

Swish. Swish. Swish.

That was it for poor Jacob, and the inning was finally over.

But the A's didn't do any better in the second inning. Bunson got careless and walked one batter, but other than that it was a lot of swings and misses, and the Dodgers were up again.

The coach yelled, "Danny, play shortstop when we go back to the field. Bat for Kenny. And Harlan, bat now for Jenny and then play first base."

Harlan felt the sudden excitement. He knew he could hit this pitcher. He got a bat and took some practice swings.

Kenny walked over to him. "Don't do what Jacob did," he said. "Relax. Swing easy."

Harlan nodded. "That's what I'm going to do," he said, and then he took some nice, level—but sort of awkward—swings. He could hear the *ping* of aluminum on the ball already. He glanced up and saw his parents wave. He was going to do it this time.

He walked to the plate and stepped in on the left-hander's side. He tried to be calm, but his heartbeat was echoing inside his batting helmet.

The first pitch seemed to float up to the plate. Harlan had to wait . . . and then he slammed it.

Or did the ball pass through his bat?

Somehow he had missed. *"Steeee-rike,"* the umpire barked.

"Just meet it," Kenny yelled.

Okay. Harlan took a deep breath and waited for the pitch.

It was fat as a volleyball and just waiting for him.

Harlan slashed at it.

And missed again.

This couldn't be happening! Everyone on the bench was yelling for him to settle down. Everyone except Bunson. Harlan looked over and saw him laugh.

This was it. Harlan would get this one.

Nice and easy. Nice and easy. He could do it.

"Hey, batta, batta, batta . . . *swing*," the A's yelled.

And Harlan swung . . . at a pitch that was in the dirt.

He stood at the plate for a few seconds, still wondering what had happened, and then he trudged back to the dugout, trying not to look at anyone—especially not at Bunson, who was laughing right out loud.

"You'll get a hit next time," Kenny said.

Harlan told himself that his friend was right. He would get another chance, and he would prove what he could do.

But as he sat down on the bench, Bunson said, "Hey, Harlan, maybe you ought to move to Paseo so you can play for the A's. They don't know how to swing a bat either." He laughed and looked around, but only his buddy Danny laughed with him. "Or just *quit*. That's one way you could help the team."

Brian Waters said, "Lay off, Bunson."

And Kenny whispered to Harlan, "Don't

pay any attention to Bunson. Get a hit next time and show him."

"That's what I'm going to do," Harlan said. But he wondered. Maybe Bunson was right.

★ 2 ★

Crash!

The A's finally got three quick outs, and the Dodgers headed back onto the field.

Harlan had his mind made up. He was going to do well at first base. He would prove to Bunson that he could play.

But Bunson needed no help with the first two batters. They were at the bottom of the batting order and they were small. Bunson fired strikes right on by them. Bunson was burning, his face red and his hair in his eyes. He must have looked mean to those A's batters.

He was acting cocky, too. "Hey, kid, you have to swing the bat once in a while if you want to get a hit," he yelled as the second batter carried his bat back to the dugout.

"That's enough of that stuff," Coach Wilkens yelled.

Bunson's mouth had already gotten him in plenty of trouble with the coach—even though the season was just getting started. But the guy didn't seem to learn.

He glared at the next batter, the little leadoff man, and grinned. He fired the ball hard and down the middle.

The batter took a good cut and popped the ball up. Harlan watched it climb into the sky right over his head. "I've got it,' he called, and then he moved toward the pitcher's mound as the breeze took the ball in that direction.

"I've got it," he kept calling, but a voice inside his head was shouting even louder, *Don't drop it. Don't drop it.*

Suddenly he realized the ball was drifting away from him. He took a couple of quick steps and lunged. The ball was almost in his glove when . . . *wham.*

Harlan was on the ground before he knew

what he had run into. But it only took a second to realize that he had slammed into Bunson, who was also going after the ball.

And the ball was rolling away somewhere.

Harlan jumped up and looked around, but Jeff Reinhold had hurried in from second and grabbed the ball.

"Time out," Coach Wilkens yelled.

Harlan spun around and saw Bunson roll over and gasp, "You idiot. You broke my ankle."

Bunson grasped his leg and pulled his knee to his chest. His face was red with pain.

The coach dropped down next to him and took hold of Bunson's leg. "Let me have a look," he said.

"That idiot Sloan ran right into me."

"Just be quiet."

Harlan stood a few steps away. Maybe the ball should have been Bunson's. Maybe this mess *was* his fault.

The crowd was very still. Even the A's players were quiet.

A man from the crowd who said he was

a paramedic came out on the field and knelt down by Bunson. He checked his ankle carefully. Finally he said, "I don't think it's broken."

"We better get it X-rayed," Coach Wilkens said. "Are his parents here?"

Harlan had never seen Bunson's parents at a game. Kenny's dad yelled that he would take Bunson to the hospital. He came out onto the field, and he and the paramedic helped Bunson up.

Bunson looked over his shoulder and said, "You've messed up my whole season, Sloan. I hope you're happy."

The coach stepped in front of Bunson. "Wait," he said. "Harlan called for it—loud and clear. If you had stayed away, he would have caught it."

"No way," Bunson growled. "I heard him call, but he never would have caught it. That's why I went after it."

"That's enough," the coach said.

The men carried Bunson off the field.

Harlan went back to first base. The coach was right. He had called for it. But maybe he wouldn't have caught it. Maybe Bunson was right about that.

Harlan felt sort of sick. Without Bunson they would probably never have a chance for the championship.

The coach called Eddie Boschi in from left field to pitch. The batter was the girl who played shortstop for the A's. She hit the ball hard but on the ground toward Jeff at second base. Jeff scooped it up and flipped it to Harlan.

But Harlan took his eye off the ball.

It bounced off his glove and rolled down the first-base line toward home plate. Billy Bacon ran after it, but the runners ended up on second and third.

Eddie and Billy both yelled to Harlan not to worry. But Harlan saw Danny Sandia shake his head in disgust.

Harlan socked his glove a couple of times and told himself he had to keep his head in the game. But the next batter hit a bouncer right at him. He got his glove down, but the ball ran up his arms and bounced off his chest.

Harlan jumped forward and grabbed at the ball, missed, grabbed again, and then spun around. Eddie had charged over to cover first. But Harlan threw the ball too hard, right on past Eddie.

It rolled down the line in right field.

By the time little Brian Waters ran it down from right field, both runners had scored and the batter had gone to second.

"That's okay, Harlan," Coach Wilkens yelled. "Just relax now and play ball. We're okay."

But Harlan felt terrible. He had always believed he would be a great ballplayer someday, but now he was beginning to wonder.

The next batter struck out and the Dodgers were finally out of the inning.

Some of the players told Harlan to forget it. But Harlan heard Jeff say to Danny, "The coach should have let him play in the minor league. He's not ready for Little League majors."

Jeff had something to say about everything. Harlan knew not to pay attention—but he couldn't help himself right now.

Things didn't get a whole lot better after that. Harlan dropped a couple more throws at first, and he struck out again.

Jacob didn't do any better. He struck out too, and he misjudged a fly ball that led to another run for the A's.

It didn't matter much. The rest of the team did fine. They scored four more runs and ended up winning 20 to 3.

That was good, of course, but Harlan heard players talking about the coming games. What if Bunson was out for the season?

After the game the coach talked to the team. He explained to everyone what he had told Bunson. The ball had been Harlan's. Infielders, not the pitcher, were supposed to handle pop-ups.

"And listen," he said. "I know the young guys got nervous and didn't do their best tonight. But you all remember what that was like. They'll be fine. They need your support. And they need a little more experience. That's all."

Harlan hoped that's all he needed.

The rookies walked home together and

they talked about the game. "Wow, Kenny," Jacob said, "you had four RBIs again and your first homer. What a game!"

"I started out okay, but I had bad swings my last two times up. I grounded out both times."

"At least you didn't strike out," Harlan said.

"I did in the last game. That happens, you guys. You're going to get some hits. Don't worry about it. Don't think about the bad stuff that happened. Remember the good things."

But Harlan *was* worried. He didn't want to get down on himself, but he couldn't think of any "good things."

The boys were waiting at the only stoplight in town. A big noisy truck rolled by. "Neither one of us got run over by a truck," Jacob said. "That's one good thing." He tried to laugh.

Yeah, but Bunson did, Harlan thought.

"What's the matter, boys? Did you get beat tonight?"

The boys turned around.

Dr. Phillips, a woman who knew every kid in town—and had delivered most of them—was smiling at them.

"No. We won," Jacob said. "Twenty to three."

"That's great. I read in the paper that you also won your first two games."

"Yup. This is three in a row now," Jacob said.

"Then why don't you sound happy?"

"We're the rookies on the team," Harlan said. "Kenny's doing great, but Jacob and I . . . aren't doing so well."

"You will," Dr. Phillips said. "It's a tradition here in Angel Park. We produce great baseball players. I think it's because there's nothing else to do." She laughed.

But Harlan didn't laugh. She was right. Baseball was the biggest thing in town. Great players were the heroes. He still wasn't used to the idea that maybe he would never be one of them.

BOX SCORE, GAME 3

Angel Park Dodgers 20 Paseo A's 3

	ab	r	h	rbi		ab	r	h	rbi
White 3b	4	3	3	4	McConnell ss	3	1	1	0
Boschi lf	4	2	3	2	Boston lf	2	1	0	0
Sandoval ss	4	3	2	4	Bessant 3b	1	0	0	0
Bunson p	3	3	3	5	Sullivan cf	3	0	0	0
Malone cf	2	1	1	1	Santos 1b	2	0	0	0
Roper 1b	1	1	0	1	Smith c	3	1	1	0
Reinhold 2b	3	2	2	2	Watrous p	2	0	1	0
Bacon c	4	2	2	1	Oshima 2b	1	0	0	0
Waters rf	3	3	2	0	Trout rf	2	0	0	0
Scott lf	2	0	0	0	Chavez cf	1	0	1	1
Sloan 1b	2	0	0	0	Powell 2b	1	0	0	0
Sandia ss	2	0	0	0	De Klein 3b	1	0	0	0
ttl	**34**	**20**	**18**	**20**		**22**	**3**	**4**	**1**

Dodgers 5 11 0 0 4 0—20
A's   0 0 2 1 0 0—3

★ 3 ★

Blasting Away

The next morning at school Harlan looked for Bunson. When he finally spotted him coming into the building, Harlan's stomach took a turn. Bunson was on crutches.

Harlan thought about avoiding him, but he had to know. He walked up to Bunson and said, "Is it broken?"

Bunson stared at him as though Harlan were a gob of fungus. "No," he said. "But I have to use crutches for a week and probably miss two weeks of playing. Is that good enough for you?"

Danny Sandia was with Bunson. "You're happy, aren't you?" he said to Harlan. "With Rodney out, you get to play more."

"I'm sorry," Harlan said. In a way, he felt like telling Bunson—and Danny—to shut their mouths. But that wouldn't help.

"You just better hope we don't lose the championship because of this," Bunson said. He hobbled away on his crutches.

Danny followed him like a little shaggy-dog puppy.

By Saturday Harlan was feeling a lot better. He was starting to remember the good things he had done in Wednesday's game. He had taken level swings; he just had to relax and meet the ball. He had improved his footwork at first base, too. He just had to follow the ball right into his glove.

The town paper had printed a nice article about the Dodgers' game. It mentioned the homers. It even described Bunson's injury, but it didn't say that a clumsy rookie had run over the top of him. Maybe one of these days Harlan would read a story about a big hit of his own.

As the game got going, the Dodgers had no problem with the Mariners' pitcher. He was a little faster than the A's pitchers, but he was wild. He would throw a couple of pitches for balls, then he would take something off the next one and bring the ball down the middle.

And the Dodgers were blasting away.

In the first inning the Dodgers got three runs, and in the second, four more.

Kenny was pitching and doing fine. He had trouble with his control in the first inning and walked a couple of guys. One scored on an error. But in the second and third innings, he got the Mariners out in order.

Bunson watched from the bleachers. He sat behind the dugout—squinting and looking mad—but he didn't have much to say.

Eddie Boschi led off the bottom of the third. He hit a pop-up that should have been an easy out, but three Mariner infielders waited for each other to catch it. It plopped on the grass and Eddie was on.

"Line drive," Eddie yelled back to his dugout. "I pounded that one." He waved his long arms over his head.

The players laughed, and Jenny yelled, "You lucked out."

But Jacob was sitting on the end of the bench, broadcasting the game as usual, talking like a grown-up instead of a freckle-faced nine-year-old. "Yes, fans, Boschi just *bashed* one. The Mariner infielders all ducked when they saw how hard that ball was hit. It was a long shot—over halfway to second base."

He switched voices. "That's right, Frank. It was hit so hard it turned to mush. It's all over the shortstop's fingers."

"That wasn't mush," Billy Bacon yelled out. "It was a cow pie. I sure hope he doesn't lick it off his fingers."

Smack.

Kenny hit a shot by the pitcher that went for a single.

"Be careful out there," Henry White yelled to the pitcher. "You're standing in a bad place."

And so it kept going. The Dodgers were pounding the ball and having fun.

Danny drove in Eddie with another single. Malone got on on an error, and then Jenny hit a ball in the right-center gap that went for a triple and cleared the bases.

Jenny took off her helmet and waved it at Eddie. "Now that's a real hit," she yelled. Harlan could see her big eyes flashing as she laughed, and then she pushed the helmet back down over her ponytail.

But before the inning was over Eddie got another chance, and he hit a drive to right field that went for a double and drove in two runs.

Seven runs scored and the Dodgers were up 14 to 1. Harlan could hardly wait to get in there and take his swings. He just knew he could get a hit.

The coach had Eddie go in to pitch, and Jacob took over in right field. That meant Kenny came out of the game. He sat down by Harlan. "You can hit this guy," he told him.

Harlan nodded. Those quiet eyes of Kenny's and the confidence in his voice really did make Harlan think he could do it. And just then the coach said, "Harlan, you bat for Jenny next inning."

Harlan slapped hands with Kenny and said, "This is it."

But the inning took a while. Eddie was trying some of his "secret" pitches. He had about twelve different grips that were for curves or drop pitches—or something fancy.

The trouble was, every pitch seemed to float up to the plate about the same—slowly. Eddie looked like a crane or a stork, all legs and wings, and his pitches didn't fool anyone.

By the time the inning was over the Mariners had gotten four runs and left the bases loaded.

Harlan was psyched to get some runs back for the Dodgers. He got a bat and waited on deck. Malone was up first.

But something had changed.

The Mariners had a new pitcher. He was a short kid, kind of flabby, but he fired the ball a lot harder than the first pitcher. He was left-handed too, and he pitched almost sidearm. That was going to be tougher for Harlan—a left-hander himself.

"Don't worry, he's not much better," Kenny yelled to Harlan.

But Harlan's spirits sank as he watched Malone swing and miss on the first pitch.

Harlan gripped his bat and he tried to time his practice swing with the pitch.

Swish.

Sterling and Harlan both swung. Sterling missed—big, strong Sterling. Harlan wondered what he would have done. Why couldn't he have gotten a chance with the other pitcher?

Swish.

Sterling was out on three pitches. "I don't believe this," Harlan muttered to himself, and he walked to the batter's box.

The first pitch looked like it was coming right at him. Harlan stepped back only to hear a big *"Steeee-rike."*

"This kid's our best pitcher," the catcher said. "He can only pitch three innings because he pitched three on Wednesday. Did you see how that ball curved?"

The catcher had a voice like sandpaper on metal.

Harlan didn't say anything. He thought

the pitcher *had* thrown a curve. He wouldn't step back this time. But the next pitch shot past Harlan before he knew it was coming.

"Oh, yeah. He's got a fastball, too," the catcher said in the same scratchy voice.

Harlan was taking no more of this. He stepped out of the box and took a couple of swings. When he stepped in again, he pushed down his helmet and got ready. He was going to time that fastball and show this catcher he wasn't impressed.

And here came the pitch.

Harlan took a hard swing . . . and the ball finally got there.

"He has a change-up, too," the catcher said, as he tossed the ball back to the pitcher. He was laughing. The sound was like fingernails on a chalkboard.

Harlan was still standing in the box.

"Son, you're out," the umpire said.

Harlan nodded and walked back to the dugout.

From the stands he heard the voice he expected. The one that had been silent all day. "Do us a favor, Sloan. Quit now."

"Shut up Bunson," Sterling Malone said.

"Don't tell me to shut up, Malone," Bunson shot back.

"Look, if all you're going to do is sit there and give guys a bad time, why don't you just stay away from the games?"

Sterling was staring at Bunson through the chain-link fence.

"I wasn't talking to you," Bunson said to Sterling.

"I know. You don't have the guts to talk to me that way. You just smart off to the third-graders."

"I'll say anything I want. You don't scare me, Malone."

Jenny stood up and turned around. "Hey, we've heard enough of what you have to say, Bunson."

Bunson stared back at Jenny, but he didn't say a word. Harlan wondered what he was thinking.

But he knew his own thoughts: Somehow, he had to show the whole team that he was worth standing up for.

★ 4 ★

Baseball Dreams

Harlan went out to play first base. He was still talking to himself. "That pitcher was tricky. But I'll get him next time. And I'm not dropping any throws today."

The Mariners' first baseman was up to bat, and he hit a hard grounder to third. Henry White gloved it. His throw was hard and a little high. Harlan had to jump . . . *but he caught it.*

He came down feeling great.

And then he realized his foot had not come down on the bag. He took a quick stab at the base, but it was too late. The runner had already crossed.

Eddie was just looking at him. Harlan knew what he was thinking.

Harlan looked over at Kenny in the dugout. "That's okay. Good catch," Kenny yelled.

Harlan took a quick look at Bunson, but the boy was stone-faced. He didn't say a word. Maybe the players had really gotten to him with what they had said.

Luckily, Eddie got the Mariners out this time. He didn't fool anyone, but the Mariners hit a couple of easy fly balls and then a grounder for a force at second. Harlan ran back to the dugout. He didn't want to look anyone in the eye.

He heard Danny talking to Bunson. "The goof finally catches the ball, and then he forgets to step on the bag. He can't do anything right." But Bunson didn't say anything.

"Don't listen to Danny," Kenny said. "It takes time to learn a position. Jenny's been playing first for three years."

"It was tough even to catch," Harlan said.

"That's right."

Harlan was clinging to that idea. But something inside him was saying, *Maybe Danny's right. Maybe I just don't have it.*

One thing that helped was to see that other guys were having trouble with the new Mariner pitcher. Billy and Brian both struck out.

Henry got a single, however, and Eddie walked. Jacob was about to come up to bat with two men on.

"Jacob," Kenny called out.

Jacob was walking to the plate, but he turned around.

"Remember. Watch the ball. Take an easy swing."

Jacob nodded, but he looked nervous.

And on his first swing, he forgot what Kenny had said.

He stepped out of the box and pounded his bat on the ground. He was mumbling, and Harlan knew he was probably doing his radio broadcast, maybe even having his announcers tell him what to do. But his stance looked good when he stepped back in—open and relaxed—and his bat was back, ready, holding still.

And then, as though everything finally clicked, Jacob took a nice, really sweet swing and—*crack*—the ball shot off his bat.

Line drive. Right over the shortstop's head.

Base hit!

Jacob charged to first and made the turn. But the other runners held at second and third. When Jacob walked back to the bag, he was smiling and looking toward Kenny and Harlan.

He had his first hit, and Harlan knew he was happy.

"We're all going to get hits," Harlan said out loud, but inside he was a little jealous.

Danny was up now with the bases loaded. But he hit the ball on the ground and the Mariners' second baseman threw him out. No runs scored.

Harlan went back to the field. And he did okay. He made two putouts without a mistake. The infielders made good throws, so the catches were not tough, but all the same he caught them.

The worst thing for Harlan was that the game was over. He wouldn't get another chance to bat. He would have to wonder for another few days whether he would ever get a hit.

After the game, Coach Wilkens congratulated the team but then said, "The next game is with the Reds. You know how good they are. Rodney's ankle is improving, but he isn't likely to be able to play. So we've all got to do our best."

All this worried Harlan.

Kenny told him they would practice hard between games.

Later that Saturday the rookies—and some other players—took extra batting practice. Monday was regular practice, but on Tuesday after school the rookies practiced again.

Kenny put some heat on the ball, and Harlan thought maybe he was swinging better. But no matter how hard he tried, he couldn't stroke the ball the way Kenny could. What was so easy and natural to Kenny was just plain hard for Harlan.

When he got home, he did some hard

thinking. Maybe loving the game wasn't enough. Maybe he had no talent. Maybe he never would be able to play well.

That night, at the dinner table, Harlan told his mom and dad he was thinking about giving up baseball.

"What?" his dad said. "Baseball is all you ever talk about. You told me you wanted to play in the majors someday."

"Maybe I'm not good enough," Harlan said.

"How do you know?" his mom said. "You just started."

"I've played in four games and I still haven't had a hit."

"What about that bunt that won the game?" Dad asked.

"That was a bunt. I can't make it to the majors on bunts."

Mom and Dad were looking at Harlan, both of them very surprised. "Son, if there's one thing I've always noticed about you," Dad said, "it's that you keep trying, even when things are hard."

"I know. But I want to be good at something. And if it's not baseball, maybe I better start trying something else."

Harlan looked down at his plate. Just looking at the tuna casserole almost made him sick. But then, pizza wouldn't have looked any better right then.

"Son," Dad said, "in the majors I think you'll find that a lot of those guys weren't stars at the beginning. They had to work hard. Don't give up on yourself in your very first season."

"That's right," Mom said.

It was stuff that parents always said. Harlan wanted to believe it. But he pictured that ball coming, and all he had to do was hit it. Something always went wrong though. It was like a beam of light he could swing right through. And for Kenny it was sitting there like a T-ball.

"Believe it or not," Dad said, laughing, "I wasn't the superstar of cement finishers the first time I tried. It took me years to become the legend I am now."

Mom laughed, but Harlan didn't.

"Your big brother and sister both had to

work harder than most," Mom said. "Brad in baseball, and Sandy in dance. But they eventually did pretty well, both of them."

But Mom didn't understand. Harlan didn't want to do "pretty well." He wanted to make it to the top. He had always been the awkward, big-eared kid. But he had pictured himself thousands of times trotting around the bases—being a star someday.

Dad was sitting by the kitchen window. The afternoon light was shining across his face and through his thinning hair. Harlan could tell that he was thinking.

"Son," Dad said, "when I was a kid I went out for the swim team. I wanted to be a diver. I told myself I was going to go to the Olympics and dive off that high platform—do triple somersaults and all that stuff."

"Really?"

"Yup." He sat looking at the table. Harlan could tell that he was remembering. "But I quit. I tried it one year, and then I quit. I told myself I'd never make it—that it was stupid to imagine that I could."

"Do you think you would have made it if

you'd kept on trying?" Harlan asked. The question was important to him.

"Well, I don't know. Probably not. I probably wasn't that great. But the thing is, I never found out how good I could have been. Every time I watch the Olympics, I think about it and I wonder. I tell myself, 'I wish I had given it my best shot.'"

Harlan nodded.

"It's not all that important, in one sense. I like my work and I have a good family. That's what matters. But still—I just wish I'd given it a shot. I think I was pretty good."

Mom said, "That's what I mean, too, honey. Don't give up on a dream the first time things turn out to be hard. If you give it your best try and it doesn't work, look for another talent to work on. But don't give up after four games."

Harlan thought that was right. He was going to keep trying.

But in bed that night, he worried. If he messed up, the Dodgers could end up blowing their win streak. He didn't want to be the cause of their first loss.

Someday maybe he would be great. But

it wasn't very likely he'd be great tomorrow afternoon. When he shut his eyes, he saw white baseballs flying past him—*swish*. What he wanted to hear was that *piiiinnnngggg* those metal bats made.

But he only heard the swishing.

★ 5 ★

Up to Bat

On Wednesday—all day—Harlan worried about the game that night. But by game time he had a plan. He asked the coach if he could talk to him for a minute.

"Coach," he said, "I know that everybody has to play. But if a kid is sick, you can't help that. Right?"

"Yeah. Sure. Why?" The coach was looking down on Harlan with a little smile. He seemed to know what was coming.

"I think I'm getting sick."

"You don't look sick."

"Well, I'm not *too* sick. But sick enough. I'll go home. That way Jenny can play the whole game at first and I won't have to bat or anything. I think the team will do better."

"What about the Giants? You gonna be sick again?"

"Yeah. Maybe I should. And then I can practice hard and maybe do okay against the Padres and the A's and the Mariners."

"Harlan, you're not as bad as you think. In a couple of years you'll be as good as anyone. You gotta play to improve. I was a tall, skinny kid—and kind of awkward. But I got so I could play some pretty good ball."

Harlan nodded. Maybe that's what he wanted to hear anyway. Maybe he was hoping the coach wouldn't tell him, "Great idea. Go home." But he was still scared.

"And there's one other thing," the coach said. "Jenny isn't going to be here today."

Harlan gulped. "Really?"

"That's right. You're starting at first base."

Harlan walked away in a daze. Now the pressure was on.

Harlan was out taking infield practice when he saw Bunson walk into the dugout.

He was off his crutches and was walking with some weight on his foot. He even had his uniform on.

"Are you going to play?" Jeff Reinhold yelled to him.

"No. Not yet. Maybe Saturday."

Jeff looked over at Harlan and gave him that broken-toothed grin. He shrugged, as if to say, "There's no figuring this guy out."

When the players came off the field, Harlan walked over to Kenny. "What's going on with Bunson?" he asked. "How come he's sitting with us—and wearing his uniform—if he can't play?"

"Maybe he wants to be part of the team after all."

Harlan wasn't sure. But he wanted to think maybe Bunson wasn't as bad a guy as he seemed.

The Reds fans were showing up now, and they were making enough noise for three teams. They had brought a big group of parents from their little town of Cactus Hills, and the players were cocky—maybe even worse than the Giants.

They never let up riding Kenny. And he really didn't play as well as usual. He pitched all right, but he walked a few. And with a couple of Dodgers' errors and some clutch hits, the Reds got four runs.

That wouldn't have been so bad, but the Dodgers only managed two in the first four innings. The team was down 4 to 2 and couldn't afford to let any more runs score.

Harlan did fairly well at first base—except for one dropped throw—but he looked terrible at the plate. He ended the fourth inning by striking out for the second time. He was getting more frustrated all the time.

The coach was staying with Kenny all the way. And Kenny's pitching was improving as the game went along.

The first batter up in the fifth was the big left-handed first baseman. He took a ball low, and then he pulled the ball hard down the line at Harlan.

Harlan took a quick step to get in front of the ball, the way the coach had shown him. But the ball skipped up over Harlan's glove and hit him right in the belt buckle.

It dropped in front of him and he picked it up and ran to the bag.

Out!

It wasn't pretty but it worked.

One away.

Harlan was surviving.

Before every pitch he hoped the ball wouldn't come to him. He was relieved when the next batter hit an easy fly to short center field and Sterling caught it. And he felt better yet when the third batter hit a high fly to left and *Jacob* caught it. The rookies hadn't lost the game yet.

As Harlan ran in from first base he thought about the batting order. He wouldn't come up this inning—not unless the Dodgers got a lot of hits—and maybe not again in the game. He still wanted another chance, no matter what.

Henry led off the inning with a walk, but the next three batters—including Jacob— made outs, and the Dodgers were back in the field before they knew it. Things looked very bad.

Kenny got the Reds out again, and Harlan

caught a fairly difficult throw to first. He had to reach to the right-field side of the bag and he kept his foot on the base.

As the team ran in, some of the players yelled to him that he had made a good play.

He felt pretty good, but then he thought of batting.

His stomach took a turn.

He would be the fifth batter. If he did get up, it would be an important situation. He felt his heart start to pound as he thought about it. All the same he wanted to do it.

The Reds were really enjoying themselves. They were yelling at Jeff Reinhold that he couldn't hit. But they knew that wasn't true. He had two hits in the game already.

Jeff got wood on the ball again, but Harlan heard the *clunk* and knew he hadn't really connected. The ball rolled to the pitcher, who turned and waited for Jeff to run awhile, and then he flipped the ball to first.

The pitcher laughed.

The infielders for the Reds tossed the ball around the horn, and then they yelled that the game was all over. "These guys can't hit," they were all shouting.

Most of the Reds' players wore batting gloves and wristbands and had expensive shoes. Their uniforms were the fanciest in the league. They just knew they were better than the Dodgers. They *looked* better.

Harlan heard the third baseman yell to the shortstop, "This kid *thinks* he's good, but he doesn't show me a thing. I don't think he can see through all that straggly hair."

He was talking about Danny Sandia. And Danny didn't like that kind of stuff. Harlan could see how mad he was.

The first pitch was inside. Danny spun away, and the big catcher, a guy named Winter, laughed in his rasping way. "What's the matter, *kid*?"

But Danny was ready for the next pitch. He stroked it past the third baseman—the one who was so sure Danny wasn't any good.

A man on. One out.

As Billy walked to the plate, Jacob announced, "This game ain't over yet, Frank. One thing about them Dodgers, they jist don't give up."

The Dodgers liked that, and they all started yelling. Even Bunson yelled, "Come on, Billy, keep it going."

And Billy did.

He didn't hit a line drive, but he was careful about the strike zone and he fouled off a couple. He finally worked the pitcher for a walk.

That brought little Brian Waters up. Harlan was heading out to the on-deck circle. He was so scared he could hardly breathe.

The game was on the line.

Harlan knew that Brian was sick of the Reds' mouths. They started their, "Hey, batta, batta, batta." They were on their toes, ready. Brian was back in the box, coiled and ready to spring, his bat up high, almost taller than he was.

And then, *slam*.

Brian hit a shot past third base. The runners took off and were heading around to score. Harlan jumped up and started to scream. The game was all tied—

"*FOUL BALL!*" the umpire shouted.

The runners had to go back.

The disappointment was hard to take. Something seemed to go out of Brian. He did manage a ground ball to the right side, but he was thrown out easily.

Two outs.

Runners at second and third.

The Dodgers were two runs down with the runners in scoring position.

But Harlan was coming up to bat.

He bit down on his bottom lip so hard it hurt. He told himself to forget everything that had happened before.

This was it.

It all came down to *right now*.

BOX SCORE, GAME 4

San Lorenzo Mariners 5   Angel Park Dodgers 14

	ab	r	h	rbi		ab	r	h	rbi
Cast cf	4	0	2	2	White 3b	5	2	3	0
Smagler 2b	2	1	0	0	Boschi lf	3	2	2	2
St. Mary lf	2	0	0	0	Sandoval p	2	3	2	1
Antonangeli c	2	1	1	0	Sandia ss	5	2	2	1
Watson ss	1	1	0	0	Malone cf	3	2	1	0
Perez 3b	4	0	0	0	Roper 1b	2	2	2	5
Sullivan p	1	0	0	0	Reinhold 2b	3	0	1	3
Rodriguez 1b	3	1	2	2	Bacon c	2	1	1	1
Tomas rf	1	0	0	0	Waters rf	4	0	1	1
Korman c	1	1	0	0	Scott rf	1	0	1	0
Amey rf	2	0	0	0	Sloan 1b	1	0	0	0
Cisco 3b	1	0	0	0					
ttl	**24**	**5**	**5**	**4**		**31**	**14**	**16**	**14**

Mariners   1 0 0   4 0 0 — 5
Dodgers   3 4 7   0 0 x — 14

You've Got to Do It

Everyone was going crazy. All the Dodgers' players were standing up, shouting to Harlan that he could do it. "Come on, Harlan. You've *GOT* to do it," someone kept yelling.

That wasn't doing Harlan any good at all.

What was a lot worse, though, was that the Reds' players were laughing at him. "Hey, Number Ten, you can just forfeit the game now and save yourself the embarrassment," the catcher said. And then he yelled to the pitcher, "He's a third-grader. Are you scared?"

The pitcher watched Harlan step up to the plate and started to laugh. The infielders were all barking away, "Hey, third-grader, don't be scared. Manny won't hurt you."

"But he did put a kid in the hospital last year," the catcher said. "You know—a pitch can get away once in a while."

"All right, that's enough of that," the umpire said.

So the catcher crouched and gave his pitcher the sign. The pitcher nodded, still smiling, and then let fly with a hard, inside fastball. Harlan didn't back off. He took a mighty swing . . . and got a lot of air.

The whole infield started to laugh.

The smart-guy third baseman, a chunky little dark-headed kid named Gerstein, yelled to Manny, the pitcher, "Don't be so mean to this poor little kid. Give him a chance."

Harlan wasn't going to let anybody talk about him like that. He gripped the bat tight and took a fierce practice swing. He was going to knock a fence down.

"Come on, Harlan. Come through."

It was Bunson. Was he being smart?

Harlan didn't know, but he was fighting

mad. He was going to hit the ball all the way out of town and across the desert. He was going to murder the thing, smash it, destroy it—

"Time out!"

Harlan looked around. Coach Wilkens was walking down the third-base line toward him. He waved for Harlan to come over.

The coach put an arm on Harlan's shoulders. "Son, you've made up your mind you're going to knock the ball into the next county, haven't you?"

How did he know?

"Let's see if you can answer a riddle."

A riddle? Had the coach lost his mind?

"What has eighteen legs and no brain?"

Harlan turned a little so he could see the coach's face. He had no idea what the guy was talking about.

"Do you know?"

"No."

"Then I'll tell you. It's the whole Reds team."

"What?"

The coach laughed, but then he said, seriously, "Look, Harlan, those guys have their minds made up you can't hit. They aren't worried about you. And that's a big mistake."

"I *can* hit. I'm going to show 'em."

"No, Harlan. That's just exactly what you *don't* want to do. This isn't a contest to see who can use his brain the *least*."

But Harlan had no idea what the coach meant.

"Look at that pitcher."

Harlan looked out at him. The guy was standing with his glove tucked under one arm. He looked like he didn't have a worry in the world. "Come on, let's go," he said, grinning and waving when he saw Harlan look at him.

"What's he thinking right now?" the coach asked.

"He's thinking that he can throw two more pitches and the game is over."

"Exactly. That's what they're all thinking. So expect two things. Expect him not to throw too hard—since he doesn't want to

walk you and have to face Jeff. And expect
the infield to be taking it easy too, not
thinking you can do anything."

Harlan was nodding. It all made sense.

"Coach, let's get it going," the umpire
yelled.

"Okay, Harlan, so what are you going to
do?"

"Power one right past those guys before
they can—"

"No, Harlan. You're going to relax. You're
going to remember this is a game. A fun
game. And you're going to use your head.
You're going to take a nice, level, smooth
swing and poke that ball through the infield. That's all you have to do."

Harlan knew the coach was right. "Okay,"
he said.

"Take another look at the pitcher. I mean,
really, isn't it funny to look at a kid who's
turned his brain off? Go ahead, laugh at
him."

Harlan laughed. The guy *did* look funny,
standing out there like he was unbeatable.

So Harlan walked to the plate.

"You can do it," the Dodgers were yelling again.

Harlan looked at the pitcher and smiled. He told himself it was a fun game and he was about to outsmart the pitcher.

The pitcher got ready and fired again, and Harlan laid off an outside pitch. But the coach was right. Manny wasn't throwing as hard. Now Harlan was ready. He had the timing.

He saw the next pitch, followed it with his eyes until it *piiinnnnggged* against his bat, and then watched as it arched smoothly and gently over the second baseman's out-stretched glove.

For a moment Harlan forgot to run. But then he took off as hard as he could go. He hardly touched the ground, all the way to first.

The right fielder charged.

The runners were going hard. Danny scored, and Billy came flying around third and headed for home. The play might have been close, but the right fielder's throw was off line. Billy scored easily.

The score was tied.

The Dodgers weren't dead yet.

The Reds' pitcher took off his glove and threw it down on the mound. And then he gave it a kick.

Harlan looked at the Dodgers' dugout. His teammates were going nuts. They were jumping all over the place—and all over each other.

Harlan grinned with those big teeth of his, and then he looked up at the bleachers. He saw his mom and dad standing up, waving, and he thought of the talk he had had with them the night before. Maybe he *could* learn to play this game!

Across the diamond Coach Wilkens was nodding and pointing to his head. Harlan knew what that meant. He nodded back. But he couldn't help laughing when he thought of the riddle—eighteen legs and no brain.

"What are *you* laughing at?" the first baseman said. "You just lucked out. I'll bet you don't get another hit off Manny all year."

Harlan knew that might be true, but he couldn't stop laughing.

And then he saw the most surprising thing

he had seen all day, all week—maybe in his whole life. Everyone in the Dodgers' dug-out was waving and yelling and cheering for him, but Bunson, of all people, was stand-ing on one foot, sort of hopping up and down. And then he shouted, "You did it, Sloan. I knew you could do it."

★ 7 ★

Last Hope

════════════════════════

"Keep it going, Henry," Harlan yelled. He was feeling great, standing on base the way he had wanted to all year. But he also knew the game was only tied, not won. He wanted to be the guy who scored the winning run.

And for a moment it seemed it might work out that way.

Henry drove a single up the middle, and Harlan went all the way to third. He was just 60 feet from home.

Eddie Boschi came back into the game to replace Jacob. He got two strikes on him before the pitcher got a little wild and walked him.

That gave Kenny the chance to win the game.

But Kenny hadn't had a hit all day. He just wasn't swinging the bat very well. He hit the ball on the ground again—an easy roller to short.

Harlan ran hard, hoping for a bad throw to first, but it wasn't to be.

Extra innings.

Things were complicated for the Dodgers now. Kenny had pitched his allowed six innings, and Eddie would have to come on to pitch. The coach moved Kenny to shortstop and Danny to Eddie's position in left field.

But Bunson walked over to the coach. Harlan heard him say, "I could probably pitch, if you want me to. I can't push off too well, but I think I can still throw harder than Eddie."

"No, I don't think so," Coach Wilkens said. "You better give it a few more days."

But in a few minutes, the whole team was wishing the coach had made the switch. Eddie walked the first batter. He was fidgeting and looking into his glove, probably trying his "secret" grips.

The coach yelled to him to throw strikes and forget about the grips.

He did throw a strike, but the Reds' center fielder, a long-armed kid, really got around on it. He drove it all the way to the fence in left field. Danny got to the ball fast and made a good throw home, stopping the runner from scoring, but now there were runners on second and third with no outs.

The next batter hit the ball hard but right at Kenny at shortstop. Kenny spotted the runner dashing for home and threw to the plate in time to cut the run off.

The Dodgers were still okay.

When the next batter popped up in foul territory, Harlan went after it. He almost overran the ball, but he stuck his glove out behind himself and made the catch. Then he spun around and watched the runners, so they wouldn't try to advance.

Harlan felt great. The catch wasn't pretty, but he had come through again, and with two outs maybe the Dodgers could get out of the inning without any damage.

But Eddie seemed to lose the plate again. He walked the next batter on four pitches. The bases were loaded.

The next batter was ninth in the order. He was the size of somebody's little brother. Harlan thought for sure they could get him.

All the Dodgers started chanting, "Batta, batta, batta," and the crowd—both teams' supporters—was yelling all at once.

And then . . . *BAM*.

The little kid hit the ball hard. Brian had been playing him close in right field. He charged the ball and made a good throw. The runner from third scored but the play was close on the second runner—until the ball got away from Billy Bacon. Two runs scored, and two guys were still on base.

The Dodgers were in deep trouble all over again.

Eddie was able to get the next batter on a ground ball, but the damage had been done.

The Dodgers yelled to each other that they were okay. They could get those runs back.

As Harlan feared, the Reds had another good pitcher. All the same, Sterling walked and Jeff hit a single.

The Dodgers weren't giving up.

All the players were yelling to Danny that he could do it. The Reds were yelling that he couldn't. The fans were making lots of noise, too. Harlan almost wanted to cover his eyes, he was so nervous for Danny.

But Danny hit one.

A line drive . . . right at the shortstop.

One out.

When Billy hit a weak roller to second and was thrown out, the Dodgers' players kept yelling, but Harlan could tell they were starting to doubt they could do it again.

Harlan walked out to the on-deck circle. His team needed two runs to tie, three to win—the same as before. It was still possible, but it was hard to think they could pull off another miracle.

What Harlan feared most was that he

would have to bat—with the game on the line again.

"Don't go away, fans," Jacob announced. "The game ain't never over 'til the last guy is out."

The Dodgers all cheered.

But they sounded nervous. They yelled to Brian that he had to do it.

Harlan was thinking. An idea was coming to him: He had seen it all in a World Series game. It was even a Dodgers game—the big-league Dodgers.

Brian was patient with the pitcher, looking for something he could really hit.

He finally got the pitch . . . but not the hit. He slapped a bouncer to the left side. The pitcher jumped off the mound and gloved it.

That was that.

He spun and threw to first.

WILD.

He had hurried more than he needed to and threw the ball in the dirt. The ball rolled past the first baseman. Sterling scored, and the Dodgers were still alive.

But Harlan was up again.

It was all up to him—one more time.

The Reds had been fairly quiet as they had gotten themselves deep into trouble, but now their cockiness came back. They began to yell that Harlan didn't have a chance— not twice.

"Wait a minute," Harlan suddenly yelled. "Ump, time out. I need to talk to my coach."

Harlan ran to Coach Wilkens.

He stopped in front of him and took a deep breath. "Why don't you put Bunson in as a pinch hitter?"

"I can't do that," the coach said. "He has to play in the game. Two innings."

"I know. But if he can drive in a run, he could go in and pitch. He said he could do it. If he doesn't drive in a run, he plays four innings in the next game, to make up for the two he didn't play this time. That's what the rule book says."

"Yeah, I know. That's true. But I don't think he can run."

"If he can hit the ball out of the infield and make it to first, the game is tied, or maybe won. All he has to do is trot to first the best he can. At least he won't strike out. He never does. And sometimes . . . I do."

"I don't know, Harlan." But the coach was thinking. And then he turned to the dugout. "Rodney, come here a second."

Bunson limped out. He even tried to run a little.

"I can play," he was saying as he reached the coach. "Do you want me to bat?"

"I guess so. But don't try to run hard on that ankle. Take your swing, and if you get the ball out of the infield, just make it to first and stay there."

Harlan was looking at Bunson. "You can hit this guy," he said. "Go do it."

"Thanks," Bunson said, and he limped toward the bat rack.

The coach walked over to tell the umpire that Bunson was now batting for Sloan.

★ 8 ★

He's Out?

Bunson tried not to limp as he walked to the batter's box, but the Reds knew Bunson, and they knew he was not planning to play. They began to needle him about not being able to run.

Harlan could sense what they were really feeling. They all knew how well Bunson could hit. And with the tying run in scoring position, they had no margin for error. They had to hope he really *couldn't* run.

Or that he couldn't put enough weight on his foot to swing well.

And on the first pitch that's exactly what happened.

Bunson swung hard, but awkwardly, and then he grunted and hopped on his good foot.

It had hurt him to swing, and everyone could see it.

The Reds picked up their chatter. They were sure they had Bunson now.

He took a pitch inside, and then he swung hard again on the next pitch. But once again, he looked like his swing was all wrong. He actually slipped and his bad ankle went out from under him. He ended up on his seat.

This brought a lot of laughs from the Reds.

"Are you okay?" Coach Wilkens yelled.

"No, he's not," the third baseman shouted, and then all the Reds picked up the chant. "Are you okay, Bunson? Are you okay, Bunson?"

Rodney got up and brushed himself off. He moved awkwardly as he favored the ankle, but he stepped back in and set himself.

Harlan could see that Bunson was mad, and he was afraid that wouldn't help any.

"This is a dramatic moment, ladies and

gentlemen," Jacob announced. "I have to remember the 1988 World Series, when Kirk Gibson came up to bat in the last inning with the game on the line—and the same kind of ankle injury. I think you all remember what he did. He knocked the ball *out of the park!*"

"*Yeah!*" the Dodgers all yelled, but Harlan didn't think they really believed it. Bunson had looked pretty bad on those two pitches.

And then Rodney swung at a bad pitch and struck . . . or did he hold up? He had tried to stop his swing.

All the Reds cheered, but the umpire hadn't called strike three.

The pitcher charged toward the plate. "He's out. He's out," he was screaming. "He swung and missed."

"No, son, he didn't go around," the umpire said. "The count is two and two."

"But he—"

"Get back to the mound and pitch."

The Reds were furious, but the pitcher went back to the mound. He took his sign, nodded, wound up, and fired.

And this time Bunson swung hard.

And connected.

He hit a fly ball, long and deep.

The left fielder went back and back.

"To the fence!" Jacob screamed.

The left fielder waited . . . waited . . . and then leaped.

But the ball was beyond his glove and . . . *"OVER THE FENCE!"*

The Dodgers went nuts. Runners were rolling around third and coming home to score. But poor Bunson was making the slowest home-run trot of all time. He was limping, almost walking, but he was pumping both arms in the air and screaming, "We did it. We did it."

Harlan ran out of the dugout with everyone else.

As Bunson rounded third, just hobbling along, everyone joined him and ran with him to home plate. But no one bumped him. They didn't want to hurt that ankle.

"We did it," Bunson was still yelling. "We came through when we had to."

Harlan didn't know whether anyone else

had noticed it or not, but Bunson wasn't saying "I did it."

Once all the celebrating was over and the Dodgers had walked across the middle of the diamond and slapped hands with the Reds, Coach Wilkens had his usual talk with the players.

"I was proud of all of you today," he said.

"Especially Bunson," Jeff yelled out.

"Well, sure. He came through, and he was brave just to go out there."

Some of the guys cheered. They were still in a celebrating mood.

Coach Wilkens waited, and then he said, "But remember, we wouldn't have gotten to the seventh inning if Harlan hadn't come through for us."

Another cheer went up.

"But that's still not what pleased me most. I had the feeling we came together today. I have the feeling we're a team now."

The coach lowered his voice a little. "Harlan was thinking of the team, not himself, when he asked me to put Rodney in.

And Rodney was thinking of the team when he agreed to give it a shot. I heard all of you cheering for each other today. We're pulling together now. And that's what it's going to take."

"We're going all the way this year," Jeff yelled.

That brought the biggest cheer yet.

"Well, I hope so," Coach Wilkens said, "but we were very fortunate to win today, and pretty lucky to get that win against the Giants. We're going to have to play better baseball if we're going to keep winning against teams like that. And remember, everyone's going to be gunning for us now. We've got to improve faster than the rest."

"Coach?" Brian Waters had his hand in the air.

"Yeah. What is it, Brian?"

"Could I be . . . excused?"

"Well, just a second. I wanted to—"

"I really have to . . . be excused." He pointed to the distant men's room.

All the players cracked up, and so did the

coach, but then he said, "That reminds me. I've got soda pop in the van. You're *all* excused."

That got another big cheer.

The whole team jumped up and ran for the van. All but Brian. And Bunson. He lagged behind as he limped across the park.

Harlan thought this was the time to talk to him. He turned and walked back, and then he said, "That was a great clutch hit."

"You came through, too," Bunson said.

The boys didn't say any more than that, but Harlan knew that things had somehow changed.

When Harlan reached the van, Kenny and Jacob were waiting. They wanted to know what Bunson had said, and they wanted to tell Harlan, one more time, what a great game he had played. And then Harlan heard his dad's voice.

"I'm planning to take all the rookies who have had at least one base hit this season out for pizza," he said. "Do you guys know any?"

They all three turned around and

grinned. And suddenly Harlan realized all over again that the pressure had finally ended. He had his hit now, and he was going to get more.

He turned to his two buddies and stuck his hand out. They all knew what that meant. They jumped up for their favorite flying *triple* high-five.

And then Harlan jumped and gave his dad a high-five too. And when he came down, he got a big hug.

"Don't give up your dreams yet," Dad told him.

"I won't," Harlan said. "Don't worry. I won't."

BOX SCORE, GAME 5

Cactus Hills Reds 6   Angel Park Dodgers 8

	ab	r	h	rbi		ab	r	h	rbi
Gerstein 3b	4	0	0	0	White 3b	3	0	3	1
Alfonsi ss	2	1	0	0	Boschi lf	2	0	0	0
Schulman lf	4	1	1	0	Sandoval p	3	0	0	0
Winter c	1	2	0	0	Malone cf	3	1	0	0
Mendelsohn cf	3	2	3	2	Reinhold 2b	4	2	3	0
Tovar p	3	0	0	0	Sandia ss	4	2	2	1
Rutter 1b	3	0	0	0	Bacon c	3	1	0	0
Trulis rf	1	0	1	2	Waters rf	2	1	0	0
Young 2b	3	0	1	2	Sloan 1b	3	0	1	2
Higdon rf	1	0	0	0	Scott lf	1	0	0	0
Bonthuis ss	1	0	0	0	Bunson p	1	1	1	4
Lum p	1	0	0	0					
ttl	**27**	**6**	**6**	**6**		**29**	**8**	**10**	**8**

Reds   1 0 3 0 0 0 2—6
Dodgers 0 2 0 0 0 2 4—8

League standings after five games:

Dodgers	5–0
Reds	4–1
Giants	3–2
Padres	2–3
Mariners	1–4
A's	0–5

Third-game scores:

Dodgers	20	A's	3
Padres	12	Mariners	10
Reds	9	Giants	5

Fourth-game scores:

Dodgers	14	Mariners	5
Giants	9	A's	8
Reds	15	Padres	0

Fifth-game scores:

Dodgers	8	Reds	6
Giants	12	Padres	7
Mariners	8	A's	3

DEAN HUGHES has written many books for children including the popular *Nutty* stories and *Jelly's Circus*. He has also published such works of literary fiction for young adults as the highly acclaimed *Family Pose*. When he's not attending Little League games, Mr. Hughes devotes his full time to writing. He lives in Utah with his wife and family.

ENTER THE ANGEL PARK ALL-STARS SWEEPSTAKES!

- The Grand Prize: a trip for four to the 1991 All-Star Game in Toronto
- 25 First Prizes: Louisville Slugger Little League bat personalized with the winner's name and the Angel Park All-Stars logo

See official entry rules below.

OFFICIAL RULES—NO PURCHASE NECESSARY

1. On an official entry form print your name, address, zip code, age, and the answer to the following question: What are the names of the three main characters in the Angel Park All-Stars books? The information needed to answer this question can be found in any of the Angel Park All-Stars books, or you may obtain an entry form, a set of rules, and the answer to the question by writing to: Angel Park Request, P.O. Box 3352, Syosset, NY 11775–3352. Each request must be mailed separately and must be received by November 1, 1990.

2. Enter as often as you wish, but each entry must be mailed separately to: ANGEL PARK ALL-STARS SWEEPSTAKES, P.O. Box 3335, Syosset, NY 11775–3335. No mechanically reproduced entries will be accepted. All entries must be received by December 1, 1990.

3. **Winners will be selected, from among correct entries received, in a random drawing conducted by National Judging Institute, Inc., an independent judging organization whose decisions are final on all matters relating to this sweepstakes. All prizes will be awarded and winners notified by mail. Prizes are nontransferable, and no substitutions or cash equivalents are allowed. Taxes, if any, are the responsibility of the individual winners. Winners may be asked to verify address or execute an affidavit of eligibility and release. No responsibility is assumed for lost, misdirected, or late entries or mail. Grand Prize consists of a three-day/two-night trip for a family of four to the 1991 All-Star Game in Toronto, Canada, including round-trip air transportation, hotel accommodations, game tickets, hotel-to-airport and hotel-to-game transfers, and breakfasts and dinners. In the event the trip is won by a minor, it will be awarded in the name of a parent or legal guardian. Trip must be taken on date specified or the prize will be forfeited and an alternate winner selected. RANDOM HOUSE, INC., and its affiliates reserve the right to use the prize winners' names and likenesses in any promotional activities relating to this sweepstakes without further compensation to the winners.**

4. Sweepstakes open to residents of the U.S. and Canada, except for the Province of Quebec. Employees and their families of RANDOM HOUSE, INC., and its affiliates, subsidiaries, advertising agencies, and retailers, and Don Jagoda Associates, Inc., may not enter. This offer is void wherever prohibited, and subject to all federal, state, and local laws.

5. **For a list of winners, send a stamped, self-addressed envelope to: ANGEL PARK WINNERS, P.O. Box 3347, Syosset, NY 11775–3347.**

Angel Park All-Stars Sweepstakes Official Entry Form

Name:_____ Age:_____
                    (Please Print)

Address_____

City/State/Zip:_____

What are the names of the three main characters in the Angel Park All-Stars books?

_____